Table of Contents

Chapter 1: Secret Surprises 5

Chapter 2: A Misunderstanding 12

Chapter 3: Party Planning 18

Chapter 4: A Quick Getaway 26

Chapter 5: Hurt Feelings 34

Chapter 6: Getting Ready 41

Chapter 7: The Big Reveal 48

Chapter 8: Best Friends Forever 57

The Birthday Surprise

Adapted by Tracey West

SCHOLASTIC INC.

ISBN 978-0-545-60589-2

12 11 10 9 8 7 6 5 4 3   14 15 16 17 18 19/0

Printed in the U.S.A.   40
First printing, January 2014

Chapter 1: Secret Surprises

Briiiiiiing!

The final bell of the day rang in Heartlake High. Classroom doors burst open and students rushed out, excited that it was Friday.

Stephanie and her friends had just finished their last-period history class. Andrea did a happy twirl in the middle of the hallway.

"School's out for the weekend, girlfriends. Yes!" she cheered.

"Oh my gosh, I'm *so* happy it's Friday," Olivia agreed.

Even though the girls shared classes together, the weekend was when they really got to hang out and have fun.

Andrea did another little twirl and held her arms out wide. "No school. No rules. So cool!"

Her friends' eyes suddenly got wide.

"Andrea . . . behind you," Olivia whispered.

Andrea slowly turned. Their history teacher, Mr. Arkin, was standing right there.

"Oh, hi, Mr. Arkin," Andrea stammered. "I was just saying . . . um . . . that I can't wait for Monday's history test. In fact, I'm off to study right now!"

The teacher raised an eyebrow. *"Mm-hmm,"* he said. Then he walked away, shaking his head.

Andrea sighed. "He's going to call on me in class on Monday. I just know it."

"Oh, but Monday is still two days away," Stephanie said with a wave of her hand. "What should we all do together this afternoon?" She pointed to a nearby bulletin board with fliers hanging on it. "In no particular order: puppy-sitting? Art exhibit? Maybe a rock concert?"

Stephanie expected her friends to all be as excited as she was. But to her surprise, the girls glanced at one another nervously and shook their heads.

"Um, I can't. I have karate class," Emma said.

Stephanie's face fell. "Oh, you do?"

Emma nodded. "Sorry, Steph. I really have to practice. My side kick looks more like I stepped on a banana peel." She demonstrated by kicking her left leg high in the air.

"Hi-ya!" Emma cried. Then she lost her balance and fell backward.

Her friends cringed.

"*Oof.* She does need practice." Mia nodded.

"And maybe some light first aid," Andrea teased.

Emma jumped up. "I'm okay! But I've got to go."

"Me, too. I have horses to train," Mia said quickly.

"And my voice teacher is waiting," Andrea added.

Olivia shuffled her feet. "And, um . . . Aunt Sophie needs help at the vet clinic. If only cages would clean themselves."

Stephanie was disappointed. All day long she had been looking forward to hanging out with her friends. But she didn't want them to see that she was upset.

"Oh, no worries. I'm totally booked, too," she fibbed. "I don't know *what* I was thinking with all this fun stuff for us to do. I have to check on the bunny I rescued."

"Oh, okay, bye!" Andrea, Mia, Emma, and Olivia quickly hurried away.

Stephanie watched them go. She couldn't help feeling a tiny bit hurt. She and her friends always hung out on Friday afternoons. They hadn't mentioned any other plans before.

Stephanie shook her thoughts away. *I'm sure we'll have fun tomorrow,* she told herself. *After all, tomorrow's my birthday!*

✳ ✳ ✳

Outside, Mia, Olivia, Emma, and Andrea
breathed sighs of relief.

"I'm glad we were able to get away from
Stephanie," Andrea said.

"Me, too," agreed Mia.

The friends smiled at one another.

"Now we can plan her surprise birthday party!"
Emma exclaimed, her green eyes shining.

The four friends had been talking about throwing Stephanie a big surprise birthday bash for days. It wasn't easy keeping their plans secret. But it was the only way to surprise her.

Olivia motioned for the others to follow her. "Come on," she said. "Let's go to the tree house. We have a lot of work to do."

They had so much to plan—and Stephanie's birthday was tomorrow!

Chapter 2: A Misunderstanding

***

A short while later, Stephanie strolled through downtown Heartlake City. Cradled in her arms was the bunny she had rescued, named Daisy. The little rabbit had fluffy white fur and a soft pink nose. For Stephanie, it was bunny-love at first sight. Now Daisy needed a nice, comfy rabbit house.

"I'm sure the Pet Parlor will have something perfect," Stephanie said. She pushed open the shop door, and a tinkling chime sounded.

Colorful pet houses lined the walls. One house had a cute pink roof. Another had pretty flowers.

"These are definitely the right size for you, Daisy," Stephanie said. "But which one should we get?"

She looked down at the little rabbit. Daisy twitched her whiskers.

"I can't decide, either." Stephanie shrugged. "They're all nice. But none of them are perfect."

Then, through the window, Stephanie saw a karate studio across the street.

"Hey, that's Emma's karate class," she realized. "Emma knows everything about style, even pet-house style. Let's go see what she thinks."

Inside the karate studio, students in white uniforms practiced punches and kicks. Noah, a boy who taught the class, instructed them how to do the moves correctly.

"Hi-ya!" he called as he kicked a big, leather punching bag. He was so focused, he didn't hear the karate studio's front door open.

"Hi, have you seen Emma?" Stephanie asked, walking up behind him.

"Huh?" Noah asked, startled. He spun to look at Stephanie and forgot to kick the punching bag. It swung back and knocked him down!

"Oops." Stephanie cringed.

Noah laughed and jumped back up.

"It's all right," he said, brushing himself off.
"And, no, I haven't seen Emma. Her next class is on
Wednesday."

"That's weird." Stephanie frowned. "Emma said
she had class today. That she needed to practice her
side kick."

"Emma? Practice?" Noah asked, surprised. "She's
the best student I have."

"Oh, well. Thanks," Stephanie said.

Her shoulders sagged as she left the karate studio.

She was starting to get a weird feeling. Emma had definitely said she was going to karate practice, but she wasn't there. It wasn't normal for her friends to fib about what they were up to. Was something going on?

Stephanie was still lost in thought when a girl named Lacy came up to her on the sidewalk. Lacy was a pretty classmate in their grade who wore fancy clothes and lived in a big house with her family. But she wasn't exactly the friendliest person.

"Who's taking karate?" Lacy asked, nodding at the bunny. "You or her?"

Stephanie shook her head. "Neither of us. Actually, I was looking for Emma. She said she'd be here, but she isn't."

"Huh. And I thought that you two were friends," Lacy said.

"I'm sure it was just a misunderstanding," Stephanie replied.

"Of course," Lacy said as she walked away. But she didn't sound convinced.

Stephanie sighed. She wasn't sure if *she* believed it herself. Why would Emma lie about karate class? She had never lied to Stephanie before.

"Come on, Daisy," Stephanie said. "Let's go home."

Chapter 3:
Party Planning

A few blocks away, Olivia, Mia, Andrea, and Emma were relaxing in Olivia's tree house. The tree's big leaves shaded them from the warm afternoon sun. A curious squirrel skittered along one of the branches in search of nuts.

"Hmmm." Olivia cupped her chin in her hands. "Where should we have Stephanie's surprise birthday party? It's got to be someplace cool."

The friends all thought hard.

"Cool . . . pool," Emma said slowly. "Hey! What about Heartlake City Pool?"

Olivia's brown eyes lit up. "A pool party! That's a great idea!"

Andrea grinned. "I'm feeling that!"

Olivia started to tick off items on her fingers. "Let's see . . . We'll need guests, a cake, presents, decorations . . . Oh, man, we've got a lot to do!"

"Stephanie usually does all that stuff," Emma pointed out.

Her friends knew that she was right. Stephanie was a natural leader. She loved to organize all their plans.

"We can totally handle it," Andrea said.

Then she noticed Mia out of the corner of her eye. Mia was holding an old, black top hat and staring at it intently.

"What are you doing?" Andrea asked.

Mia held up the hat. "Working on a magic trick for the party," she said. "And I've finally got it."

"Show us," Emma urged.

"Sure," Mia said. "Watch as I pull a rabbit from this ordinary black hat."

She waved her right arm dramatically.

"Abracadabra!" she cried. Then she put her hand into the hat . . . and pulled out the curious squirrel!

"Eeeeek!" Mia shrieked. The other girls cried out, too, as the squirrel darted away.

"Is that part of the trick?" Emma asked.

"Oh, I get it," Olivia said. "It's a *comedy* act!"

The girls giggled. Mia blushed, embarrassed.

"No, it's not," she said. "I guess I need more practice."

"You'll get it, Mia," Olivia assured her.

"Speaking of practice, let's rehearse our dance," Andrea said. "It's got to be perfect for the party."

She climbed down the tree-house ladder and landed on the grass. Her friends followed her. Andrea had shown them the dance once, but they were still learning it.

Emma, Olivia, and Mia lined up next to one another. Andrea pressed a button on her boom box and cranked up the volume.

"Five, six, seven, eight . . ." she counted. "Now, left!"

Mia and Emma took a step to the left . . . and Olivia took a step to the right.

"Your *other* left, Olivia!" Andrea called out.

Olivia took another step to the right . . . and landed on Mia's foot!

"Sorry," she said. She closed her eyes, trying to concentrate. "Left, left . . . right, right."

Soon Olivia got into the groove with her friends.

"See?" she said, smiling. "This is why we have to practice!"

They all laughed.

Little did they know, Stephanie was walking down the road right past Olivia's house. She really missed being with her friends. It felt so strange to not be together.

Suddenly, Stephanie heard music echoing from the tree house. The pop-song lyrics *"Me and my girls, we're best friends forever!"* echoed down the block.

Stephanie walked closer and gasped. Andrea, Emma, Olivia, and Mia were all together. They were dancing and having fun—without her!

Stephanie ducked behind a bush. "Why am I not a part of this?" she asked herself, annoyed. "They must have texted me."

She took out her phone. "Yeah, one text!" she said. Then her smile faded. "From Mom. About chores."

She peeked up over the bush again. *They're dancing, and they didn't invite me,* Stephanie thought. *Does this mean I'm not their friend?*

Part of her wanted to march right up to them and ask what was going on. But the other part of her felt a little afraid. What if they really *didn't* want to be her friends anymore? What if they had left her out for a reason?

They must not have wanted me to be with them, Stephanie thought sadly. *I should get out of here.* She hurried away.

The moment Stephanie was around the corner and out of sight, a boy skateboarded down the road toward Olivia's house. He had wavy brown hair and blue eyes. He skidded to a stop in front of the tree house and hopped off his board.

"Looking good, girls," he said, giving them a thumbs-up.

"Thanks, Jacob." Olivia waved, smiling.

"I got your text about Stephanie's party," Jacob said. "What can I do?"

"Keep it a secret," Emma replied.

"I mean besides that," Jacob said, rolling his eyes.

"Can you be in charge of lights?" Andrea asked. "They're over there in that box."

"I'm on it," Jacob said. "I helped stage a concert one time so I'm pretty good with lighting."

"Awesome!" said Olivia. "Let's get to work. We still have a lot to do!"

Chapter 4: A Quick Getaway

The girls made a list of everything they needed for the party. Olivia and Mia volunteered to pick out a great present for Stephanie.

They went to the Pet Parlor downtown. Inside, a white poodle wagged its tail.

"Aren't you cute?" Mia asked, scratching the dog's head. The poodle barked.

Just then, a young sales clerk walked up to them. "Hi," she said, with a friendly smile. "Can I help you?"

"We're looking for a birthday present for our friend Stephanie," Mia said.

"We want to get a house for her bunny, Daisy," added Olivia.

The clerk led them to the row of bunny houses Stephanie had looked at earlier that afternoon.

"We have lots of choices," the clerk said.

Mia and Olivia looked at each house carefully. They both liked the one with the purple roof. It had a pretty pink gate across the front.

"This one's great!" Mia said.

"I love it!" agreed Olivia.

"Does it come with a bed?" Mia asked.

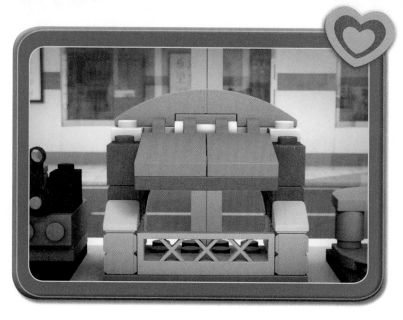

"Is it wired for sound?" asked Olivia.

"Or a pillow?"

"Or maybe lights?"

"Is there a shelf for brushes?"

"Um . . ." the clerk stammered. She looked overwhelmed. "Sorry, it only comes like you see it."

Mia frowned. "Oh."

But Olivia's eyes lit up. "Hey, maybe we could put in our *own* special touches."

Mia nodded. "Yeah! Customize it! Stephanie will love that!"

They smiled at the clerk. "We'll take it!"

Soon Mia and Olivia were walking out the front door with a big white gift box wrapped with a red bow. They were so excited. This was going to be the perfect gift for their friend!

Just then, they heard a familiar voice.

"Mia! Olivia!"

The girls stopped in their tracks. Stephanie was running toward them from down the street.

Mia and Olivia panicked. If Stephanie caught them, they would have to explain the present they were carrying. And if they did that, they would ruin the surprise!

"Pretend we didn't hear her!" Olivia whispered urgently. "Hurry!"

They quickly ran around the block and hid behind the pet shop building.

Stephanie tried to catch up to them. But when she turned the corner, her friends were nowhere to be seen.

"I guess they didn't hear me," she said sadly.

Olivia peeked around the wall of the building and saw Stephanie walking away.

"*Phew!* Close one!" she said.

"Yeah," Mia agreed. "That could have been a disaster."

Little did they know, to Stephanie, it *did* feel like

a disaster. Her friends lied about having plans. They had danced at the tree house without her. Now Mia and Olivia didn't even stop when she called out to them. Why were her friends acting this way?

She walked down to Lake Heart and sat on the dock, dangling her legs over the edge. Swans glided on the peaceful water. The sun was starting to set. Stephanie sighed and threw a pebble into the lake.

Suddenly, she heard a soft whinny behind her. Stephanie turned and saw Lacy trotting up on a horse from the Heartlake Stables.

"All alone?" Lacy asked. "Where are your friends?"

"What friends?" Stephanie replied bitterly. "They lied to me. And then I saw them having fun and dancing at the tree house."

"Maybe it's your dancing," Lacy teased.

Stephanie sighed. "It's just weird for them to suddenly act this way."

Lacy didn't reply for a moment.

"Friends don't often give reasons for moving on," she said finally. "They just do."

"Oh," Stephanie said. Lacy seemed to know what she was talking about.

"Want to go for a ride?" Lacy asked. "It helps."

Stephanie shook her head. "Thanks, but I'm going to figure this whole thing out. Especially since tomorrow's my birthday."

Lacy shrugged. "All right." She trotted away.

Stephanie turned back to the lake and tossed in another pebble.

I only want one thing for my birthday, she thought. *My friends back!*

Chapter 5:
Hurt Feelings

Saturday morning, Stephanie put her plan into action. If her friends were really avoiding her, then there was no choice but to play detective and see what they were up to!

Wearing a pair of dark sunglasses, she hid behind the fence next to Olivia's house. A moment later, the front door opened. Olivia came

out of the house, carrying an oversize beach bag.

"Have fun at the pool," Olivia's mom called.

"Thanks, I will," Olivia replied. Then she headed down the sidewalk.

Stephanie waited until Olivia was about a block away before following after her. She hid behind cars and trees in case Olivia turned around. So far, so good.

Olivia strolled downtown and stopped at a photo booth. Emma, Mia, and Andrea were waiting there. All four girls went inside and closed the curtain.

Stephanie dashed across the street and hid beside the booth, listening.

The girls didn't know that Stephanie was spying on them. They squeezed in, giggling. Andrea leaned toward the camera, blocking her friends.

"Does my hair look all right?" she asked.

"It looks good from the back," Emma said. "But, uh, can we be in the picture?"

Andrea laughed and moved back with her friends.

"Everyone smile!" Olivia called out.

"*Cheeeeeese!*"

There was a *beep*, and the camera flashed.

"Glamour pose!" Andrea cried.

The girls made their best model faces.

Flash!

"Silly pose!" Mia called out next. She stuck out her tongue. Her friends all made funny faces, too.

Flash!

They left the photo booth, laughing. Stephanie watched as they all walked in different directions. She decided to follow Emma.

Emma headed past the City Park Café, crossed

a busy street, and walked down to a row of shops. Stephanie trailed close behind.

Suddenly, Emma paused. She thought she had heard something.

Before Emma could spot her, Stephanie quickly ducked into a clothing store and put on a floppy hat so she looked like a mannequin.

Curious, Emma walked back to the store. The cute clothes in the window caught her eye, so she went inside. Stephanie blended right into the window display and Emma didn't see her.

Emma browsed around for a minute. "These shirts are cute," she said to herself, holding up a pretty summertime top. Then she shook her head. She had an important job to do. There was no time for shopping! She left the store.

Stephanie jumped out of the window display and hurried to catch up. A few blocks later, she spotted Emma coming out of the bakery, carrying a big box.

This was Stephanie's chance. Her friends were *definitely* up to something and purposefully weren't including her. She took off her sunglasses and marched up to Emma.

Emma gasped. "Stephanie! Oh, hi. What's . . . up?" She sounded nervous.

"Back at ya," Stephanie said.

Emma tried to act casual. Stephanie's birthday cake was inside the box she was holding! But she couldn't let her friend know that.

"Just, you know, did some shopping," Emma said. "Got a little snack. . . ."

Stephanie eyed the large box. "A *little* snack?"

Emma laughed nervously. "Skipped breakfast. And now I'm heading to . . ."

"Karate class?" Stephanie asked. She thought she could catch Emma in another lie.

"No, the library," Emma said quickly.

"But don't you get the feeling that today is . . . special?" Stephanie hinted.

Emma gasped. "You're totally right!"

"I am? You mean, you know what today is?" Stephanie asked, immediately brightening. Maybe Emma remembered it was her birthday after all!

"Yes!" Emma replied. "I volunteered to help at the Art Exhibit today!"

Stephanie's face fell.

"If I hadn't run into you, I would have forgotten," Emma continued. She inched away. "Thanks a million, Stephanie!"

Emma quickly walked off, and Stephanie's heart sank.

She could forgive her friends not including her yesterday. But today was her birthday! How could they be so mean?

Chapter 6: Getting Ready

When Emma arrived at the pool, the other girls were already busy setting up. Andrea tied bunches of colorful balloons to the lifeguard tower. Mia and Olivia hung a big, pink banner with Stephanie's name between two light posts. And pretty flowers ran up the poles by the snack bar.

"Where do you want these, Andrea?" Jacob called out. He was carrying the box of tangled lights.

"Over there, behind the hot tub," she replied, pointing.

"Got it," Jacob said cheerfully.

Emma put the cake on a big table. Olivia was placing other yummy snacks there, too.

"I ran into Stephanie at the bakery," Emma said.

Olivia gasped. "Did she find out about the surprise?" she asked, anxious.

Emma shook her head. "No, but I felt terrible making excuses to her," she said. "Stephanie looked kind of upset. I think she could tell something was up."

"I know, but it'll all be worth it when we surprise her," Olivia promised.

Across the pool, Mia set her magic hat on a table. She closed her eyes. The squirrel from the tree house watched her. Would she get the trick right?

"Abracadabra!" Mia said. She opened her eyes. A shimmering bubble floated out from the hat.

Mia smiled. It wasn't a rabbit, but it was still nice. And definitely better than a squirrel!

Then . . . *pop*! The bubble burst. The squirrel chittered and scampered away.

Mia sighed. "Gotta keep practicing, I guess," she muttered.

Up in the lifeguard tower, Andrea tried to connect her boom box to the pool's speakers.

"What about this one?" she wondered. She plugged in one of the cords.

Screech! Feedback wailed from the speaker. A little puff of smoke popped up.

"Looks like Andrea might need some help," Olivia told Emma. "I'd better go check."

As Olivia was heading over to the lifeguard tower, she passed Jacob. He had successfully untangled all the lights and was carefully stringing them between two light posts by the hot tub.

"Hey, Jacob," Olivia called. "Actually, the lights go on *that* wall." She pointed to the opposite end of the pool.

Jacob looked over his shoulder. "Are you sure?" he asked. "Because Andrea said . . ." But Olivia was already out of earshot.

"Aargh," he complained, taking the lights back down. He carried his ladder over to the wall on the far side of the pool.

Meanwhile, up in the tower, Olivia and Andrea got the speakers working. Andrea pressed PLAY on her boom box, and pop music floated through the air.

Olivia and Andrea climbed down and headed over to Mia and Emma.

"Those speakers are kickin'!" Mia exclaimed.

"They are, aren't they?" Olivia agreed proudly.

The girls high-fived. Then they looked around the pool. The balloons, streamers, and banners all looked great.

"Everything's just about ready," Andrea said.

Emma frowned. "Except Jacob's putting the lights in the wrong place." She turned and called out to him, "Jacob, the lights go over there."

"No, they go behind the hot tub," Andrea said.

"You mean behind the slide," said Mia.

Olivia shook her head. "You're all wrong. They—"

A loud whistle pierced the air. It was Jacob, whistling through his teeth.

"The lights are here, they stay here!" he said firmly. "I'm not moving them again."

The girls looked at each other and shrugged.

"Fine," said Emma.

"What's up with Jacob?" Mia asked, loud enough for him to hear.

Jacob slapped a hand to his forehead. "Girls! I simply don't get them!" he cried.

Olivia turned to her friends. "I'm so excited. People will be here any minute!"

"I can't wait to yell, 'Surprise, Stephanie!'" Emma clapped her hands.

Olivia's eyes suddenly grew wide. "Hey. Just how does Stephanie know to come here again?" she asked.

Andrea gasped. "Did we . . . skip a step?"

"You mean, like invite the guest of honor?" Mia asked. "Then, yep."

Emma groaned. "Oh, no! We forgot to invite Stephanie to her own surprise party!"

Chapter 7:
The Big
Reveal

On the other side of town, Stephanie walked into a ballet studio. Inside, dancers in white leotards and pink tutus danced to classical music. Lacy was there warming up. She stretched her right arm gracefully above her head.

Stephanie headed over to her. "I got your text," she said. "You wanted to see me?"

Lacy brightened. "I wanted to give you this," she said. "Happy Birthday."

She held out a yellow mixing bowl with a ribbon around it. Inside were two colorful mixing spoons.

"I heard you like to bake," Lacy said, giving the bowl to Stephanie.

Stephanie couldn't hide how happy the gift made her. For the first time today, she felt like someone actually cared that it was her birthday!

"Thanks for remembering!" she said with a huge grin. "I'm glad *someone* did."

She looked happily down at the bowl. Lacy had even gone to the trouble of finding out what Stephanie liked. The gift really meant a lot to her.

"Say, maybe we can make a birthday cake or something," Stephanie suggested. "We could head back to my house. I'm sure my mom has some cake mix in the pantry. It will be fun. And, after all, it seems like a good day for it."

"You mean, make it *together*?" Lacy asked eagerly. Stephanie had never asked to hang out with her before. She was always so busy with her other friends.

"Sure," Stephanie said.

"Okay!" Lacy agreed. Then she paused. "Unless you have other plans, because . . . I might have other plans."

Stephanie shook her head. "I don't have plans."

"Yeah, me neither," Lacy admitted with a grin.

The girls laughed. Stephanie was happy that she had a friend to spend her birthday with. But there was still one big problem that needed to be fixed.

"First there's something I have to do," she told Lacy. "Come with me."

Over at the pool, Olivia, Andrea, Emma, and
Mia were panicking. Boys and girls were arriving,
ready for the party to begin. But they couldn't start
without the birthday girl!

"Guests are coming, people!" Andrea said
anxiously.

"Think," Olivia said. "How do we get Stephanie
here without ruining the surprise?"

"We could tell her it's *my* surprise birthday party," Emma suggested.

Mia shook her head. "She knows when all of our birthdays are."

"We need to do something cleverer," Mia said. "What if an animal needed rescuing?"

Andrea ran toward the pool. "We could say a dolphin is drowning in the pool!"

"Do you know how ridiculous that sounds?" Mia asked.

"Yes, but I'm starting to freak out!" Andrea cried.

"Me, too," Emma agreed. "We don't want the party to be a total bust!"

"You mean, like, our friendship?"

The girls turned to see Stephanie standing by the entrance. She looked angry. Lacy was behind her, leading her horse.

"Stephanie!" they cried.

"Friends don't lie to each other," Stephanie shot back. It felt good to get the words out. "And then

they don't go off and dance and take secret pictures together."

"Stephanie, you misunderstood—" Olivia tried to explain.

"Oh, really?" Stephanie asked. "Well, friends don't have swim parties at the pool without you, or . . ."

She pointed to all the beautiful decorations around the pool. And as she did, her voice slowly trailed off. There were balloons, and streamers . . . and a big banner with her name on it.

"Huh?" she asked.

"Surprise!" her friends yelled. "Happy Birthday!"
They ran up to Stephanie and hugged her.

"Happy birthday . . . to me?" Stephanie asked.
She was stunned.

"Yes, you!" Andrea said.

"We've been planning the surprise all along," Mia explained.

Stephanie's eyes grew wide. Everything was starting to make sense. "So that's what all the sneaking around was about?" she asked.

"Yeah," Andrea replied. "You seriously didn't think we were trying to unfriend you, did you?"

"Of course not," Stephanie answered. Then she looked down. "Well, actually . . . yeah."

"Please," Mia said, waving her hand.

"We would never do that!" Emma promised.

Andrea opened her arms wide. "We just wanted you to have the best birthday ever!"

Stephanie looked around. The pool was beautiful. Great music filled the air, and all of her classmates from school were there.

"Oh my gosh, it's amazing!" she breathed. She couldn't believe it. Her friends weren't trying to ditch her after all. They were trying to surprise her!

She hugged them all again. "Thank you so, so much! Just promise me one thing."

"What's that?" Olivia asked.

Stephanie grinned. "Don't ever do it again!"

Chapter 8: Best Friends Forever

This is such an incredible birthday surprise! Stephanie thought. *I didn't lose my friends after all. And now there's this great party!*

Stephanie was so relieved that she didn't notice Lacy inching away from the group.

Lacy had really been enjoying her afternoon with Stephanie. For a moment, she thought that they might even become friends. But now that Stephanie had her real friends back, Lacy was sure she wouldn't want to hang out anymore. She decided it was best for her to head home.

Stephanie was about to go off when she spotted Lacy out of the corner of her eye. "Wait here one moment," Stephanie said to the girls. "I'll be right back." She ran over to Lacy.

"Where are you going?" she asked.

"Oh, you know, plans," Lacy lied. "Sorry. I told you I couldn't stay long."

Stephanie smiled and held out her hand. "Look, I know you're totally busy, but can't you stay anyway? As a favor?"

Lacy hesitated. Then a smile crossed her face. "Well, I guess so," she said taking Stephanie's hand.

"Come on, open your presents!" Olivia said excitedly.

Stephanie sat down at the poolside tables where all her birthday presents were stacked.

Emma handed her a purple frame with a photo inside. It was the picture of the girls making silly faces in the photo booth.

Stephanie laughed. "Great picture! I'll put it in my room. Thanks, you guys."

Then Mia brought over the big white box with the red bow Stephanie had seen them carrying the other day. Stephanie lifted the lid and gasped. The pieces for a beautiful rabbit house were tucked inside!

Emma grinned and held up one of the blocks. "Let's put it together!" she said.

The girls snapped all the pieces into place. The purple roof had a HAPPY BIRTHDAY sticker on it, and they added that next. Then they attached a pink front gate. Emma handed Stephanie a bowl with carrots in it.

"For Daisy," she said.

"Aw, you guys thought of everything," Stephanie said happily.

"There's more," Olivia said with a grin. She and Mia each placed a bunch of roses on both sides of the roof.

"Daisy's going to love it!" Stephanie exclaimed. "I wish I could have brought her."

Emma and Andrea winked at each other. The surprises for Stephanie weren't over yet!

Mia jumped up on top of a table, wearing the black top hat.

"Ladies and gentlemen, if I can have your attention," she announced. Mia took off her hat and held it out. "While this may look like an ordinary hat, I promise you, it isn't," she said. She held the hat in her left hand, and waved her right hand dramatically.

"Abracadabra!" she cried.

Mia looked inside the hat ... and frowned. She turned it upside down, but nothing came out. She tapped on the bottom of the hat, and still nothing.

Then Mia smiled. She was just acting! She reached into the hat ... and pulled out a fluffy white rabbit!

"Daisy!" Stephanie cried happily.

The bunny jumped into Stephanie's arms, and Stephanie hugged her pet. "You guys, this party couldn't be any cooler!" she exclaimed.

"Oh, but it can!" Jacob called out. He ducked behind the snack bar and put his hand on a light switch.

"Three . . . two . . . one!"

He flipped the switch, and dozens of lights

flickered on all across the pool. Since the girls couldn't decide where to put them, Jacob had put them everywhere! The pink, blue, and green lights glowed softly against the night sky. The party guests *ooh*ed and *aah*ed.

"They're beautiful!" Stephanie breathed.

Jacob walked up to Olivia.

"I like what you did," Olivia said.

"Well, I *am* the Light Master," Jacob joked, and they both laughed.

"You guys are the best!" Stephanie told her friends.

Andrea pressed a button on the boom box. "It's time to get this party started!" she cried.

Everyone let out a cheer. The girls ran over to the side of the pool, and Andrea grabbed Stephanie's hand. Then the five friends lined up. A pop song pumped out of the boom box.

Stephanie realized that this was the dance she had seen them practicing. She looked at Andrea and smiled. She knew just what to do.

She joined the girls as they danced along to the music.

Best friends forever,
forever and ever.
No matter what happens,
we stick together.
Me and my girls,
we're best friends forever.

Stephanie looked at each of the girls. They *were* her best friends forever—and she knew she would never doubt them again.